Kohkum's Kitchen

Written by
Mark Thunderchild

Illustrated by
Amanda Melnychuk

 FriesenPress

One Printers Way
Altona, MB R0G 0B0
Canada

www.friesenpress.com

ISBN
978-1-03-917589-1 (Hardcover)
978-1-03-917588-4 (Paperback)
978-1-03-917590-7 (eBook)

1. JUVENILE FICTION, FAMILY, MULTIGENERATIONAL

Distributed to the trade by The Ingram Book Company

This book was written in part inspiration from
My Kohkum Mary Thunderchild, it was her love and
knowledge that cultivated my large community-like
extended family.

In Kohkum's kitchen, everyone is hard at work as the family gathers, including many of her children and her grandchildren.

Kohkum has made some fresh stew for everyone!
"Mmmm," the children say!

"What's the occasion?" Auntie Mary asks with a mouthful!

"Mushum brought home a moose yesterday and we have lots of fresh meat!" says Kohkum.

Mushum smiles and says "Not just me, my young hunters helped as well!" As the bigger kids smiled with pride.

The next morning, all of the children go to Kohkum and Mushum's house before school. They pick up their lunches and say goodbye to their grandparents.

On the bus the children are giggling and excited about their lunches, so much so that they argue why the stew is so good!

"Kohkum has the best recipes and makes the best bannock That's why the stew is so good!" Allyanna says as she is holding up some bannock.

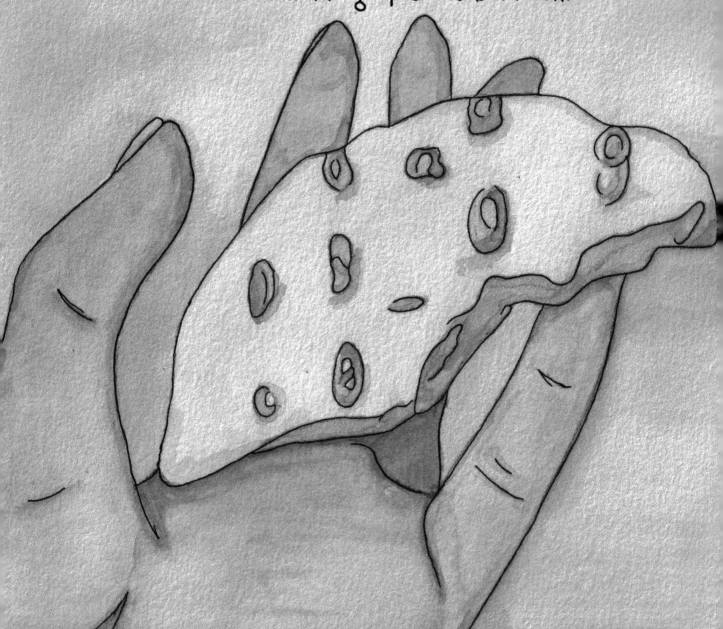

"Mushum's moose meat makes the stew the best, we hunted it like the old ways and gave thanks to the Creator for nourishing us! That's why the stew is so good!"

Dominic says.

This arguing went on all day.
The children just could not decide
why their food was sooo good.

They even got their friends involved. "Here try this!" as
Allyanna gave Jessica a bite of her stew and bannock.

Jessica opened her eyes wide,
"WHY IS THE STEW SOOO GOOD?"

Not one of them could convince Jessica if it was Kohkum's kitchen or Mushum's moose meat that made the stew so good.

They just all agreed that it was very, very good.

Finally, when they got home, the children went straight to their parents and asked them.

WHY IS THE STEW SOOO GOOD?

"Well children, as your family gets bigger, the more love you have to give, so Kohkum and Mushum after all they have learned and all they have loved, put the knowledge and love in the food they feed us. So, they're both why the stew is sooo good!"

Printed in the USA
CPSIA information can be obtained
at www.ICGtesting.com
LVHW071825251023
761973LV00003B/58